Catherine Rayner

Five Bears

MACMILLAN CHILDREN'S BOOKS

Bear was quietly walking along, just being a bear.
A nice bear by all accounts,
but a bear all the same.

When Bear saw . . .

A bear!
A bear he did not know.

"Are you looking at me?" asked Bear, suspiciously.

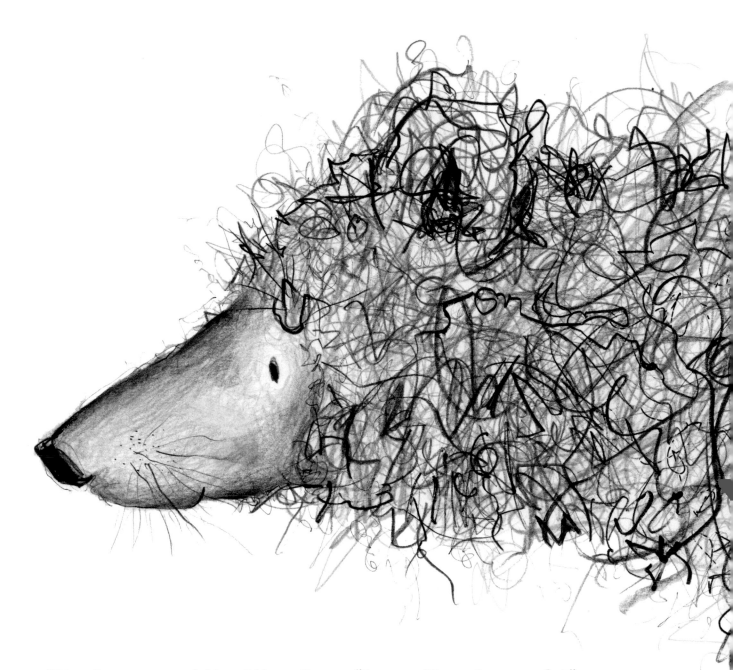

"Yes," answered the Other Bear. "I was. How do you do?"
"I'm fine," said Bear warily. "Why are you talking to me?"
"No reason," said the Other Bear. "Just saying hello.
Have a nice day!"

The Other Bear walked on.

Bear decided to follow.

Two bears wandered along at different paces,
thinking different thoughts, and looking in
different directions, when they met . . .

A bear!

"What do you want from me?" grunted the new bear.
First Bear looked at the Other Bear.
"Nothing," they said. "We hope you have a nice day."
"Oh!" said the Grunty Bear, looking a little embarrassed.
"Thank you. I will."

Three bears wandered along at different paces, thinking different thoughts, but now looking in the same direction, when they saw . . .

A bear!
A very big bear!

"Go away," said the Very Big Bear.
"Why?" said the three bears.
"I don't know you," said the
Very Big Bear.

"Okay then. Well, good to meet you. Have a nice day," said the three bears and they walked away.

The Very Big Bear watched them go. They seemed like friendly bears.

The Very Big Bear felt a little bit lonely and
decided to follow.

Four bears wandered along at different paces,
but they were starting to think similar thoughts
— it was pleasant to be with other bears.

And they were all looking in exactly the same
direction when they saw . . .

A bear!
A stuck bear! Up a very large tree.

"Leave me alone," growled the Stuck Bear,
"I'm fine by myself."

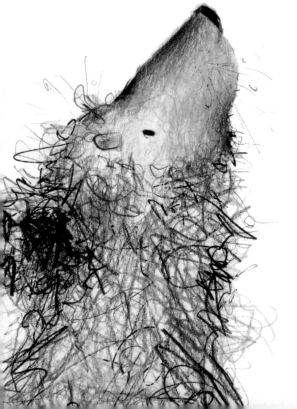

But a Stuck Bear clearly needs help.

Four bears stood together, looking up and thinking exactly the same thing.

They talked, they planned and they encouraged the Stuck Bear until, at last, they helped that bear down.

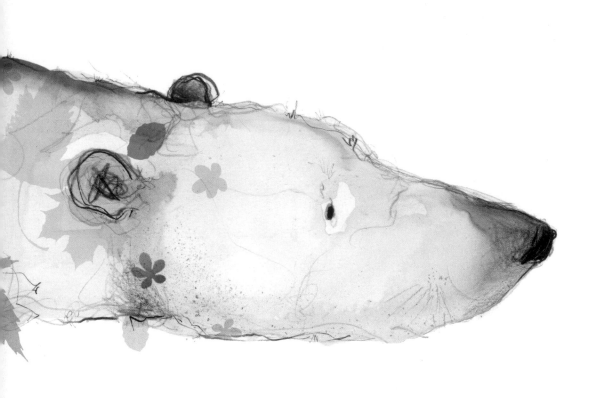

"Why did you help me?" said the
Unstuck Bear.

"Some things are hard on your own.
Nothing more!" said the four bears
as they calmly walked away.
"Have a nice day!"

Unstuck Bear thought for a while.

Then ran after them and said, "Wait! I've never actually spoken to another bear.
I didn't know if I'd like other bears. I didn't know if they would like me."

Unstuck Bear thought for a little longer, then said, "I didn't know if different bears could be friends. But you are all very different. Why are you together?"

All the bears looked at each other.
All the bears thought for a while.
All the bears felt happier than they
had in a long time.
Then they all spoke at once.

Because actually, it was simple . . .

"We all just like each other!"

And five friends walked on together.

They talked to one another.
They laughed with one another,
and they listened and they learned
about one another . . .

. . . and they all had a VERY nice day.

For all the 'Stuck Bears' out there, because
sometimes everybody needs a little bit of help.
And to Colin the bear, with my love. X
CR

First published 2022 by Macmillan Children's Books
This edition published 2023 by Macmillan Children's Books
an imprint of Pan Macmillan
The Smithson, 6 Briset Street, London EC1M 5NR
EU representative: Macmillan Publishers Ireland Limited,
1st Floor, The Liffey Trust Centre,
117-126 Sheriff Street Upper, Dublin 1, D01 YC43

Associated companies throughout the world
www.panmacmillan.com

ISBN: 978-1-0350-2969-3

Text and illustrations copyright © Catherine Rayner 2022

The right of Catherine Rayner to be identified as the author and illustrator of this work has been asserted
by her in accordance with the Copyright, Designs and Patents Act 1988.

1 3 5 7 9 8 6 4 2

A CIP catalogue record for this book is available from the British Library.

Printed in China.

MIX
Paper | Supporting
responsible forestry
FSC® C116313
FSC
www.fsc.org